THE
LOSER
LIST

TAKE ME TO YOUR LOSER

Also by H.N. Kowitt

THE
LOSER
LIST

TAKE ME TO YOUR LOSER

written and Illustrated by

H.N. KOWITT

SCHOLASTIC PRESS / NEW YORK

ISBN 978-0-545-50795-0

12 11 10 9 8 7 6 5 4 3 2 1   13 14 15 16 17 18/0

Printed in the U.S.A.   23

First printing, October 2013

For Joanne Trestrail

* CHAPTER ONE *

My heart sank when I saw the dry-erase board:

I'd been dreading it all week, ever since Coach Kilshaw had warned us there'd be an in-class competition in gym. I turned to my best friend, Jasper, who wasn't any happier than I was.

"Now guys can beat us up for school credit," I said.

"Won't they match us with someone our own size?" asked Jasper.

In my case, that meant "short." I scanned the possibilities in my gym class: Pinky Shroeder. Ethan Fogerty. Jasper. That new guy with wild black hair. None of us were in danger of being chosen "Athlete of the Year" at Gerald Ford Middle School.

"I hope you're right." I looked at the beefy jocks across the room, kids like Bruce "Bruiser" Pekarsky, "Abs" Tanaka, and Kyle Larson. They were bouncing around like restless zoo animals.

Coach Kilshaw blew his whistle.

"Today I'm assigning matchups for the tournament," he roared. "Now, you've all heard rumors about wrestling injuries — don't believe 'em. Rick Lambretta did NOT have a ruptured spleen."

Who's Rick Lambretta?

"Or spinal contusions." Coach shook his head. "Anyway, he's doing a lot better."

Jasper and I exchanged looks. Now Coach was reading off the first-round matchups: "Kirby Hammer — Quinn Romanoff. T-Bone Farrell — Luke Strohmer. Danny Shine —"

I held my breath.

"Bruiser Pekarsky," he finished.

NOOOOOOOOOOOOOOOOOOO!!!!!

My stomach dropped to my knees. The guy outweighed me by at least fifty pounds — besides, he was a Neanderthal who'd probably be out for blood! Jasper looked at me and groaned. It was the worst possible news.

For Bruiser too apparently. He frowned as he looked me up and down. "Oh, man."

When Coach was done reading off names, Bruiser and I shot over to him. "Can we switch opponents?" I asked Kilshaw. "I mean, look at us!"

Kilshaw didn't look up from his clipboard. "No changes."

"Coach," I tried again. "We don't —"

"There aren't enough heavyweights, so some of you are under-matched," he said. "DEAL WITH IT."

Bruiser cursed and pounded a beefy fist against his thigh. I bit my lip. We walked away in silence.

"Tough luck," Bruiser said. "See you Thursday."

"Yeah," I choked out.

At my locker, Jasper and I held an emergency meeting.

"Bruiser Freakin' Pekursky," I spat out.

Jasper didn't have to worry. He'd gotten paired with Phil Petrokis, a skinny tech geek. Not exactly Clash of the Titans.

"How bad could it be?" Jasper asked. "They can't let someone, like, totally whale on you. Can they?"

"I'm not doing it." I thought about Bruiser's sweaty flesh. "NO WAY."

"Yeah, but —" Jasper shook his head. "How're you going to get out of it?"

"I'll think of something I have to do Thursday," I said. "Doctor's appointment. Religious holiday. Organ donation."

* TOP THREE WORST EXCUSES FOR GETTING OUT OF GYM

1. Foosball Finger
2. Allergic to sweat

3. My brother really needs my kidney

As we passed a bulletin board, my eyes scanned the flyers. "Hold on," I said, slowing down to look. Suddenly, a word jumped out at me.

"Want to run for student council president?" I read out loud. "Info session THURSDAY, FIFTH PERIOD."

Gym was fifth period.

"That's it!" I shouted, pounding the bulletin board so hard a couple flyers came unpinned and fluttered down. "That's my excuse!"

"Perfect, except for one thing," Jasper said. "You're not running."

"It's just an info session," I said. "I could say I'm _thinking_ about running." Another image of Bruiser flashed through my mind.

Jasper squinted at the poster. "It says 'serious candidates only.'"

"It also says you can get out of class." I scribbled down the info on a Taco Dog napkin. "YESSS!"

I reached for a high five, but Jasper only tapped me.

As I walked to lunch on Thursday, someone called, "Hey, Danny." I turned around and groaned. It was Axl Ryan, the school's biggest bully.

"I heard Bruiser's going to waste you today." Axl's tone was conversational. "Wish I could see it."

"I won't be there," I shot back. "Student council info meeting. Got a written excuse."

"Really?" he asked. "That works?"

I started to feel uneasy. "I've got to go."

"You da man!" Axl shouted as I hurried away.

When the school's biggest bully compliments your deviousness, it's probably not a good sign.

The fifth-period bell rang, and I walked

into the info session like it was no big deal. As if I were a student-government type, not a comic book geek who couldn't care less about the seventh-grade class gift. Finding a desk in the back row, I dumped my backpack.

Right now I could be pinned under Bruiser Pekarsky. I remembered the look on Kilshaw's face when I went to tell him I'd be absent.

"What is it _this_ time, Shine?" he'd said with a sigh. "Sprained eyebrow? Underwear's too tight?"

Thinking about that conversation made me squirm, but it was worth it. I looked around the room to see who else was there.

* MALIBU NUSSBAUM

Reputation: Political activist
Last crusade: School Mitten
    Drive

* KENDRA
MAXTONE-COUSINS

Reputation: Butt-kisser
Last speech: "why the
   School Day Should be
   Longer"

FUTURE
DERMATOLOGISTS

* TY RANDALL

AKA: "Mr. Perfect."
Last seen: On skateboard,
   delivering meals to
   homebound seniors.

   "Raina! Da'Nise! Sit there." It was Chantal
Davis, the class diva, walking into the info session.
If she was running, that meant it was a cool
thing to do. She had a lot of power; kids liked

her sassy personality, great singing voice, and who-cares attitude. Plus they were just plain scared _not_ to like her.

I tried to sink low into my seat so Chantal wouldn't see me. She'd only give me grief, like always. Once I wouldn't let her "borrow" my good drawing pen, and she put my name on the Loser List in the girls' bathroom.

"Danny Shine?!" she shrieked. "I can't believe it. You? Running for _president_?"

Her friends giggled.

"I don't know," I muttered. "Maybe."

To my relief, Mr. Amundson walked in. Our trying-to-be-cool vice principal stood in front of the classroom, pointing his fingers at us. "As stu co adviser, I'm totally jazzed to see such a large turnout!" he said. "I count fifteen solid citizens."

Then he launched into the president's responsibilities: Lead meetings. Speak at assemblies. Attend fund-raisers. Oversee committees. Go to more meetings.

It sounded deadly.

Student council member Malibu Nussbaum read a list of campaign rules:

"No negative wording on campaign materials."

"No bribing people with candy to get votes."

"No stickers."

"The most important things to ask yourself are..." Amundson paused. "Do I have outstanding leadership skills? Am I a positive role model? Do I have what it takes to represent Gerald Ford Middle School?"

No, no, and no.

"Questions?" asked Amundson.

"You didn't say what the perks are," said

Chantal. "Extra-big locker? Front-row basketball seats? Private bathroom stall?"

"Hall passes? Free food?" shouted the crowd.

"Uh, no," Amundson said. "Being president is about what you do for _other_ people. It's fighting for things you want, like bike racks, or a vegetable garden, or —"

Suddenly, there was a commotion at the door. I looked over and saw Mrs. Lacewell, the school administrator, arguing with Axl Ryan.

Oh no. What was _he_ doing here?

"I can go — it's a free country!" snapped Axl. He turned to his best friends, Boris and Spike, nodding for them to follow. The three of them formed the Skulls, the school's only gang.

"Smells like you just want out of English class today," said Lacewell.

"No! I swear! I'm really interested in —"

"Running for president?" Lacewell arched her eyebrow.

Everyone snickered.

"Maybe." Axl sniffed.

"'Cause that's the only way you can be here," she said. "IF. YOU. ARE. TRULY. RUNNING."

"He's not running!" Axl's arm shot out.

Crud! He was pointing at me.

"Danny's just here to get out of the wrestling tournament!" Axl shouted. "He said so!"

Holy crud. Lacewell glared at me.

"Mr. Shine, may I see you for a moment?" she snapped. "Out in the hall."

Out in the hall was never a good thing. Lacewell let Axl go and ushered me out of the room, planting me in front of some lockers.

"Danny, what's all this about you missing a wrestling tournament?"

"Um —"

"You are here because you are running for president, aren't you?"

Crud.

"I'm — I was thinking about it, but —"

Lacewell's eyes fixed on me like a laser beam.

"But what?"

Choose your words carefully. "But after hearing more about the job, I don't think I'm, uh, cut out for it."

"NOT CUT OUT FOR IT?" Her eyes were blazing. "Danny, you better run, or I've been played for a fool. Together we'll go to the principal and tell him what you've been up to."

No, no, no!

Not Dr. Kulbarsh! He'd devour me like a mini-egg roll! He loved to make "examples" out of kids; his briefcase was rumored to be filled with medieval torture instruments.

I'd get his "I'm Very Disappointed" speech; he might even call my parents. NO!

"Don't go to Kulbarsh," I burst out. "I'll run."

* CHAPTER TWO *

"Look on the bright side," said Jasper. "You'll never win anyway."

I'd tracked him down at Funland, the local gaming arcade. Of course, he was right, but hearing him say it, I felt a perverse twist of disappointment. True, I didn't _want_ to be president, but it still hurt — a little bit — to think I had no chance at all.

Jasper continued. "Presidents are either Cool Table types or the kind who circulate petitions for meat-free cafeteria meals. They're never people like us." He pulled levers back and forth.

"Meaning..."

"Under-the-radar geeks who spend Saturday nights at *Comix Nation*," he said, naming our favorite comic book store.

"Okay, well, phew."

"What a drag." Jasper shook his head.

"The meeting was awful," I said. "All about 'leadership qualities,' and 'being a role model.' When I heard what you have to do, I almost barfed. Attend all school-wide events! Pep rallies! Public speaking!"

Jasper whistled.

"Can you see me overseeing the Spirit Week Decorations Committee?" I sputtered.

Jasper shook his head. "No way."

"I'm not interested in student government!" I said. "I just want to be left alone to draw."

"I hear you," said Jasper. "Who wants to go to a Safe Street Crossing Assembly?"

Nice of him not to say "I told you so."

"Look, I need a campaign manager," I said. "To make sure I _don't_ get elected. Keep me out of the limelight."

"Then I'm your man," said Jasper. "I'm great at attracting no attention whatsoever."

As if to prove his point, a big guy in a knit cap came up to us and took over the game Jasper was playing, as if he wasn't even there. Jasper just shrugged and headed to another machine.

"Strategy session tomorrow?" I asked.

"I'll bring my worst ideas," he said.

His pinky finger met mine for a secret handshake.

We met at the "Office," a janitor's supply closet, during lunch hour. Sitting on drums of

barf powder, we turned it into a "war room"
for campaign strategy.

"The first thing we need is a platform,
right?" I asked.

"Right," said Jasper. "Our own little wish list,
since it's not going to happen anyway."

"Exactly."

"If you could redesign school, what would you do?" Jasper asked.

The cliquish lunchroom scene flashed through my mind. Today I'd seen my secret crush, Asia O'Neill, sitting with the most popular kids. Of course I didn't go over and join her; it's not like just anyone could sit there.

"I'd make the cafeteria Cool Table open admissions." I smiled.

"Keep going." Jasper wrote in his notebook.

"Prom King and Queen chosen by grade point average," I said.

"I've got one," said Jasper. "Dates for the dance determined by computer matchup. Then guys like us would have a chance."

Dreaming up a geek's wish list was fun. "What else?" I asked. "Swirly-proof toilets?"

"No school sports!" Jasper's fist shot up.

"Sci-fi theme for Winter Carnival!"

We laughed. "Finally, school the way we want it," sang Jasper. "Required classes in special-effects video editing!" We liked to make low-budget horror movies, like our epic, It Must Have Been Someone I Ate.

"And Krazy Karl could be a writer in residence!" I shouted. He was the author of Rat Girl, my favorite comic.

Jasper wrote it all down in his notebook. "Now we're getting somewhere."

"Yoo-hoo in the soda machines —"

"School-wide Trivia Smackdown —"

Working on a joke campaign was actually a blast.

"You're running for class president?" Asia O'Neill's eyes widened. "Cool. Interesting. Unexpected."

I'd run into her at the library. Asia is a weird mix of things: beautiful, quirky, smart, and a tomboy. She's always surprising me with comments like, "You know, it's not that hard to repair a skateboard" or "I'd rather be home playing Garage Band." I don't know any other girl like her.

"Yeah. I'm running." My voice was low.

"That's fantastic." Her face lit up like she really meant it. "Giving your free time to help the school. I'm impressed."

"Mmh." I looked at the floor. Not a good time to say I was running a joke campaign.

"Why did you do it?" Asia asked.

So I wouldn't have to wrestle Bruiser.

"Seemed like a good idea."

I peeked to look at her library books.

"Student council doesn't have to be lame," she said. "My cousin's school had a fund-raiser called A Thousand Cranes, where students made origami birds. They raised money for a hospital in India."

"That sounds amazing," I said. Knowing I'd never be elected, I could afford to be enthusiastic.

"Isn't it?" Her eyes were shining.

She launched into a story, which I barely heard. The cherry-Twizzler smell of her hair was seriously interfering with my concentration. I mumbled something back.

"I'm so glad you like my idea." She pointed to my book. "What are you checking out?"

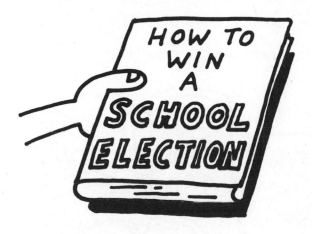

I showed her the book. I didn't mention that I planned to read the advice and do the opposite.

The first time I saw one was in the cafeteria. They were on every table.

I tossed a piece
to Jasper, and he
gave me a high five.
"WOO-HOO!"

This was great news. If Chantal was
running, no one else had a prayer. I popped
some into my mouth.

"Hey." Jasper pointed. "It's not just gum."
Chantal's name was everywhere.

How had she gotten stuff printed up so fast?

A crowd had gathered around a table. "Only
one per person," Phil Petrokis announced as

people grabbed CHANTAL: THE TIME IS NOW T-shirts.

"What are you doing here?" I asked. In addition to being the perfect wrestling partner for Jasper, Phil was a friend and fellow comic book geek.

"I'm her campaign manager and pollster," Phil explained.

"Does she even need one?" asked Jasper.

"Early numbers say she'll sweep all five homerooms," said Phil. "She polls well with Popular Girls, Almost-Cools, and Wannabes. Less well among Jocks, though Frisbee Guys are the exception. Needs more name recognition with Bookish Nobodies. They tend to back Ty Randall and Malibu Nussbaum, but who knows? My sampling has a twelve-point margin of error."

I edged over to see Chantal in campaign mode — shaking hands and talking passionately.

"We've got to make this school all it can be," she pleaded. "Professional-quality talent shows! Top choreographers! Costume budget!"

Just then, Axl swung by. Everyone stopped talking. Chantal and Axl were known enemies.

"Fancy-shmancy," Axl said, looking around and nodding. "T-shirts. Visors. Pencils."

Chantal ignored him.

"Who do you think you are?" He snickered. "Hillary Clinton?"

She turned to him with burning eyes.

"Axl, you are one sorry lowlife," she said. "You're just jealous 'cuz _you_ could never win."

People gathered around, hoping for a fight. When Axl and Chantal got together, the sparks flew fast and furious. They were the only ones not scared of each other.

Axl gave a spooky smile. "I could beat you at anything, Chantal."

"Oooooooh," the crowd murmured.

"_Not_ running for _president_." Chantal's voice was fierce. "You couldn't even qualify. You've got to have teacher recommendations!"

"Yup, even running for president." Axl smiled again. "I could beat you."

More Ooooohs.

"You can't back that up." Chantal lifted her chin.

"Yeah!" "Got that right!" "You tell 'im!" Her friends cheered. Then she went one step too far.

"You're too chicken," she added.

Then Axl got right in Chantal's face. Everyone held their breath until he broke the silence.

"Game. On."

* CHAPTER THREE *

Nothing you say matters, I reminded myself.
I had no chance of winning whatsoever.

Chantal, Axl, Malibu, Ty, and I were at the
candidates' debate in the auditorium, sitting
onstage at a metal folding table. Our moderator,
Mr. Amundson, was at the podium, welcoming
everyone. Attendance was mandatory.

Looking into the audience, I nodded to
Jasper in the third row. We both agreed the

debate was no big deal. Everyone knew Chantal would win.

Still, being onstage made my palms sweat. Being a joke candidate sounded doable in Jasper's bedroom, but now I wasn't so sure. Plus — my heart pounded faster just thinking about it — what would Asia think?

While Kulbarsh made some announcements, I leaned over to Axl. "How'd you get to run?" I asked. "I thought you had to have a certain grade point average."

Axl shrugged. "Wagman gave me a recommendation." Our English teacher was always trying to reform troublemakers. "I had to promise to bring every grade up to D-minus," he said.

"What about the 'no suspensions' rule?"

Axl scowled. "A lot of those were <u>bogus</u>. Last month? The ferret was dead before I got there."

Right.

"So..." I kept my voice low. "What have you been doing campaign-wise?"

Axl flashed an evil grin.

"Fund-raising," he said. I could only imagine.

Amundson finished announcements and turned to the candidates. "Okay, dawgs, it's go time. Hit me with your opening statements!"

We each got our turn.

Chantal

...'S about time we elected a left-handed black female Capricorn...

Ty

...greener. Electric school buses. And a sneaker recycling program...

Malibu

. . . real change. Better learning conditions, smarter budget choices. And a smoothie machine . . .

. . . a lot of ridiculous rules here. Like you can't 'borrow' someone's bike, even for short rides. Or draw graffiti on your own locker . . .

Axl

My turn! I swallowed hard.

"I'd make this school more geek-friendly," I said, taking a deep breath. "Comic book inking would be a class, like math or history. Die, Monster, Die would be screened in homerooms, instead of What Every Teen Should Know."

From the audience I heard a few laughs.

Feeling bolder, I went on. "Chess Club would have cheerleaders. Mathletes would get pep rallies.

"Popularity would be based on movie trivia knowledge," I continued.

More laughs.

"Okay, great!" Amundson said. "Let's move on to the audience questions! School budgets, curriculum issues, standardized tests?"

Dead silence.

"Someone must have a question," he begged.

Finally, Sophie De Mano stood up. "What's your position on Hippie Day?" she asked.

Amundson squinted. "What?"

"Hippie Day." Sophie looked impatient. "When you dress in sixties' clothes."

"FOR IT," declared Chantal. "I'm itching to try out Mom's old bell-bottoms."

The other candidates looked uncertain.

Malibu grabbed the mike. "I'd work with the student council to coordinate Pajama Day, Backwards Day, Hippie Day, and Twin Day."

Ethan Fogerty was next. "This is a question for Axl. What do you think of the 'three absences and you get detention' rule?"

Axl looked pleased to be asked. "I think it's dog barf," he said. "The detention room is overcrowded. You can't just dump kids there. You've got to rehabilitate them."

Amundson leaned forward. "Good questions. Keep 'em coming."

Ginnifer Baxter stood up.

"How about more school dances?" she asked. "At Highland, they have Snow Ball, Spring Fever, and Valentine's Day King of Hearts."

At the mention of Highland, our school rival, some people yelled, "They suck!"

"I'm all about dances," Chantal assured her. "With kickin' themes like Seventies Disco, Fire

and Ice, or Hollywood Nights. Not boring ol'
winter Wonderland."

  "One more question," Amundson warned.

  The new guy with wild black hair stood
up. "What makes each of you qualified to be
president?"

  "I started running to annoy Chantal," Axl
admitted. "But now I'm into it. Guys like me
don't get enough say at this school. I've got
ideas. Like, how about a graffiti art show?
Guitar Hero contest? Killa whale concert?"

His ideas weren't bad. Graffiti show —
why not?

"My opponent thinks drawing on a locker
counts as art," said Chantal. "I want to
upgrade the school, not trash it. First-rate
musicals. Ice-cream toppings bar in the
cafeteria. Bathroom stocked with scented soap,
hair gel, and body butter."

"Tell it, girl!"

"Uh-HUH!"

"Yes, indeed!"

Body butter? Jasper mouthed.

"I don't want to trash the school." Axl
shrugged. "I just don't think it's a beauty spa."

"He shouldn't be allowed to run," Chantal muttered. "Moron."

"Freak!" Axl shot back.

"Dirtbag!"

"Idiot!"

"ENOUGH!" Amundson put his hand up. He turned to the rest of the table. "Ty?"

Mr. Perfect tossed back his caramel-colored hair. He explained how, at his old school in California, he'd started a model UN, crisis hotline, and Friends of the Planet Club.

"Great." Amundson nodded. "Danny?"

My stomach lurched. I had to follow him?

I opened my mouth and stopped. Was I trying to win people over or not? Being a joke candidate was more complicated than I had thought. But I had to keep going.

"I'm a comic book geek," I said. "Types like me don't get chosen Prom King or Best Athlete. We never hear about movie outings, or that great beach party in someone's basement where they brought in real sand."

When I paused, it was pin-drop quiet.

"Geeks see things differently," I said. "They like Sustained Silent Reading Hour, and they don't care what sweater they have on. They can do strange and amazing things, like build robots and identify birdcalls. They give us Rat Girl comics and the Hubble telescope. We need their point of view."

"Woo-hoo!" some people yelled.

Huh. I hadn't meant to give a pro-geek rant, but somehow it spilled out. As their applause roared in my ears, I looked down at Jasper. He gave me a thumbs-up. All of a sudden, my chest felt lighter. Me, giving a speech!

I turned to Malibu.

She swallowed. "I'm a good listener and problem solver." She talked about creating a video yearbook, tutoring center, and High School Preview Day.

That's who SHOULD be president, I thought. But the audience seemed restless; even Amundson was tapping his knee. When she was done, he jumped up — a little too quickly — and said, "That's all the time we have. Can I get a 'what what' for these guys?"

Hurried applause was followed by a mad dash for the door. Malibu, Ty, Axl, and I shuffled offstage, but there was a mob around Chantal. "You killed it," someone told her. "Go, girl!"

Chantal had won over the audience. But looking at the rest of us, I felt kind of . . . proud. Being up there hadn't been easy. Putting myself through it was either brave or stupid.

Soon, I'd find out which.

* CHAPTER FOUR *

"Chantal's out of the race," Jasper burst out.

I was so startled I dropped my <u>Gateway to Algebra</u> book in front of his locker. Had I heard right? She'd just spent all week bragging about how she'd improve the school.

"Why did she drop out?" I asked, stunned.

"She was disqualified." Jasper was out of

51

breath. "Phil Petrokis told me. They're announcing it in homeroom."

"Why?"

"Overdue library books!" Jasper said. "Dozens of 'em. You can't run for office if you have outstanding fines."

"How much does she owe?" I tried to imagine.

"A lot." Jasper put out his hands. "More than the GDP of most small countries. And she can't pay it because she spent all her money on Vote for Chantal umbrellas and stuff."

"Hmmm." What did this mean for me?

Jasper read my mind. "Don't worry. You're doing okay among Tech Geeks and Less-Popular Girls. But Ty, Malibu, and Axl are still ahead of you, so it won't matter."

Phew.

Just then, two girls stopped right in front of us. Raina and Da'Nise — Chantal's best friends. What were they doing here? Girls like that never talked to us.

"Greetings and salutations," said Jasper, adjusting his glasses.

Raina nudged Da'Nise.

"You heard Chantal got disqualified, right?" Da'Nise said. "Well, we've got good news."

Jasper and I leaned in.

"She's endorsing you for president."

At lunch, we saw the buttons:

And the posters:

And the T-shirts:

"Way to go!" said my friend Emma.

"Lucky break!" said Kirby Hammer.

"Geeks rule!" shouted Pinky Shroeder.

Everyone knew the power of Chantal's backing. She had pushed through her own candidates for hall monitor, cheerleader, and talent show contestant.

Jasper and I slumped through the lunch line, devastated. All our best laid plans . . . ruined.

"When did she have time to change those

buttons and T-shirts?" Jasper's face was pale. "She had no right!"

"She can't just decide the election!" I shook my head.

We looked at each other, hearing how strange that sounded. What a weird position — not wanting things to go our way.

"You must be so happy," Asia O'Neill said, stopping me in the hall. "It's really happening! Next week, you could be student council president!"

"Unh..." I tried to imagine it.

"What's wrong?" Asia's eyebrows came together.

I don't want to be president. "Nothing, it's just, um —" I looked around. "Unfair to other candidates."

"She has the right to throw her support to someone," Asia said. "You <u>have</u> to get that job. Then we could do all the stuff we talked about!"

<u>What stuff?</u> I didn't even remember, but the word "we" made my pulse jump. Before I could ask, she floated off with a wave.

Marching back to Jasper's table, I set down my tray with a thud. We'd chosen an out-of-the-way spot near the recycling bins so we could talk.

"This election is really freaking me out," I said in a low, frantic voice. "We've got to put the brakes on. <u>Now.</u>"

"On it," Jasper said. "I told Phil Petrokis we need to talk to Chantal. I didn't tell him the reason."

"Why would she pick me, anyway?" I asked. "And go to all this effort?"

"Because of him." Jasper pointed.

"She doesn't want Axl to win," said Jasper.

"But it doesn't make sense." I shook my head, puzzling it out. "Why not throw her support to Ty or Malibu? Someone with a better chance?"

Jasper shrugged. "There's Phil. Maybe he'll know." He was heading straight for us.

"Hey." Phil was out of breath. "I've only got a sec. Chantal's laying low right now, but at three thirty she'll meet you at the mall. Fitting room at the Gap — third stall on the right."

"Fitting room . . . ?"

"Don't worry, it's unisex. She always has meetings there. The password is 'Pink Champagne' — her favorite gourmet jelly bean flavor."

"Pink Champagne." Jasper typed into his phone.

"By the way, the big endorsement?" Phil patted his chest. "My idea. Geek power, right?"

Jasper and I exchanged looks.

Phil pulled up his sweater to reveal his T-shirt.

"Don't thank me," he said.

"TAKE BACK THE ENDORSEMENT?" Chantal's eyes blazed. "Danny Shine, are you _crazy?_"

Jasper and I looked at the floor. I wondered if people in other fitting rooms could hear.

"Do you know what my endorsement is WORTH?" she fumed. "It's like I went and handed you the election!"

"I know. And I'm..." I nodded. "Flattered."

Horrified is more like it.

"You could actually win!" Chantal kept shaking her head. "Think about it. You already got the Loser vote."

"Chantal —" My voice felt strangled. "I'm starting to think I don't want to be president. Can't you, uh, un-endorse me?"

"WHAT?" she screeched. "All those buttons and T-shirts — it's too late! If we changed 'em again, how dumb would that look?"

"For God's sake," I begged. "It's just some stupid T-shirts!"

"And buttons. And tote bags. I was even going to do a fund-raiser for you..." Chantal sighed.

"BUT I DON'T WANT IT!" I rubbed my forehead in frustration. "Can't you throw your support to Malibu? Why ME?"

She leaned in and whispered. "Because if Axl gets beat by you, it's more humiliating. Besides, Malibu's too old-school." Chantal waved her hand. "Waste-free Wednesdays and boring stuff. We've got to kick it up a notch." She closed her eyes. "Contests, Casino Nights, Fashion Fridays..."

I made a face. "Why would I be any better?"

"Because, Danny." Chantal smiled slyly. "I can help..."

With a jolt, I saw what she was picturing.

Suddenly, it was all too clear . . .

"No, Chantal." It was time to pull out my nuclear option. I looked at Jasper. "No, no, no, no! I'm dropping out of the race. What's the worst Lacewell can do?"

"This meeting is over." Chantal stood up. She spoke calmly, like she was explaining to a young child. "Danny, you're going to stay in the race and you're going to win. And if I <u>don't</u> see your name on that ballot?"

I looked up uncertainly.

"It's <u>not</u> <u>Lacewell</u> you'll need to be afraid of." Then she shoved me against the wall and walked out.

* CHAPTER FIVE *

We had two days to turn the race around.

"This time we have to get <u>serious</u> about losing," I said to Jasper in the War Room the next day. "Put out ideas NO ONE could agree with, even geeks."

"Yup." Jasper squinted at his laptop. "We've got to be totally toxic."

"Loser Central."

"Dork-a-rific."

OPERATION NEGATIVE LANDSLIDE had begun. We paced around, trying to focus. Even though the school was full of awful ideas (Mother/Son Dance, anyone?), trying to come up with them deliberately was surprisingly hard.

"Got one." Jasper lifted up his index finger. "For the lunchroom? Turnip Tuesdays."

"Mushroom Mondays —"

"Fish Stew Fridays."

"Good." I wrote in my notebook. "Besides thinking of new bad events, we can make old ones worse. How about a barbershop quartet for Spring Dance?"

"...And for the End-of-the-Year Party Jam —"

"Classical music!" I shouted.

Once we got started, we couldn't stop. The putrid ideas just kept on coming...

Movie Nights

Field Trips

"We could suggest school clubs no one would join," said Jasper.

"Shorter vacations."

"Parent/substitute teacher conferences —"

"Bathroom Clean-Up-a-Thons —"

"These ideas stink," I said. "But just thinking them up isn't enough. We've got to get out there and nauseate people."

We stood up and did our secret handshake.

"Let's go," I said.

The next day we brought my new campaign flyers to lunch.

"Homework during vacation breaks?" Emma gasped. "Irish clog dancing instead of hip-hop? A stricter dress code???"

She was reading the new flyer. I looked around the lunch table and saw horrified looks from Sophie, Morgan, and Kendra. Jasper whispered, "See? It's working."

"What _kind_ of stricter dress code?" Sophie's eyes widened.

"Um..." What would people hate most? "Some kind of school uniform. Red blazers, white blouses. Like at military academies." I coughed.

"Geez." Sophie shook her head.

"Yodel-a-Thon? Winter Waltz?!" Emma continued reading. "These are the worst ideas EVER!"

* TOP FIVE WORST SCHOOL EVENTS

1. Accordion Hero Contest
2. Cooking with the Principal
3. Librarian/Student Football Game
4. Knit-a-Palooza
5. Battle of the Polka Bands

"What are you trying to do?" Sophie sputtered. "Make school suck _more_? You might as well suggest boy-girl bathrooms and shorter lunch periods!"

"Good ideas," I said, writing them down.

Their reaction told me our plan worked: we had convinced everyone I was clueless. It was a strange victory. When this was all over, I'd explain my strategy and reclaim my reputation. We only had to keep it up for _one more day_.

Jasper stood up. "Thanks. That's all we need."

As we left the table, Kirby Hammer grabbed me. "Hey, Danny." He held up a video camera. "Can I interview you for a candidates' roundup? We'll show it in homerooms tomorrow before election. Last chance to make your case."

Jasper's eyes gleamed. "Awesome."

My skin suddenly felt itchy. It was one thing to say goofy things to a few people in the cafeteria. But did I have the guts to act like a moron in front of the whole school? Jasper nudged me, but I pushed him away.

"Just a sec," Jasper told Kirby, then dragged me aside.

I folded my arms.

"Do you want to attend leadership conferences and promote school spirit?" Jasper hissed. "Or be a positive role model?"

I shook my head.

"Then DO THE FREAKIN' INTERVIEW!" He shoved me toward Kirby.

"Okay," said Kirby, pushing some buttons on his camera. "Stand there, next to the drinking fountain."

People stopped by to listen. I rubbed my knuckles, trying to get my courage up. Who knew that trying to act _less_ cool than I was would be even harder than trying to act _more cool_? I cleared my throat.

"There are so many ways to improve Gerald Ford," I began. "Assign more homework. Play bagpipe music over the PA. Make mall walking a school sport . . ."

"Eeeew!"

"What the . . . ?"

I talked louder, to be heard over the vomit noises. Meanwhile, Jasper handed out my new flyers.

"... and finally, I think we should post everyone's report card on the school website," I finished. "If you agree, please give me your vote."

People fled the area like it was a toxic-waste dump. When Kirby gave me a "cut" signal, Jasper patted me on the back.

Defeat was within reach.

Election day finally arrived.

Waiting to cast my vote, I kept my head down. People were in line, stuffing their ballots into a cardboard box in the cafeteria. After my campaign video aired, I was afraid to look at anyone.

Besides, my outfit was embarrassing. Jasper had persuaded me to wear the worst clothes I could think of. "It's your last chance to turn people off," he argued.

I looked up for a moment and caught Pinky Shroeder's eye. Shoot! He came over.

"Hilarious video," he said.

Huh?

"Yeah," said Ethan Fogerty. "It rocked."

Jasper and I looked at each other. What part of "I'm the Pro-Homework Candidate" didn't they understand?

"Ukulele Fest," Pinky went on. "That's a good one."

Katelyn Ogleby and Ginnifer Baxter turned around. "At first we were like, what's his problem? But Chantal explained."

"Explained . . . what?" My voice cracked.

"That you were just being funny." Katelyn turned away and dropped her vote in the ballot box. "Chantal tweeted it."

"What'd she say?"

"That that's your sense of humor." Katelyn's eyes wandered around. "Making fun of school. Once we got it, we cracked up."

I shot another panicked glance at Jasper. How many people got Chantal's tweets? Looking around, I caught a few more people smiling at me. Quinn Romanoff pointed at me with fingers aimed like guns. What else had Chantal done to "help"?

The line moved again, and suddenly it was my turn at the ballot box. I had an uneasy feeling as I reached into the slot and dropped in my vote for Malibu.

"Good luck, Danny," whispered Asia as we filed into the auditorium.

"Thanks," I mumbled, embarrassed.

We were on our way to the Friday Assembly to hear election results. Thinking about Asia seeing my campaign video made me wince. I tumbled into a seat next to Jasper while Kulbarsh waited onstage for the audience to quiet down.

Finally, the last armpit fart died.

"Before I announce the winner, I want

to talk about..." He lifted his chin. "The losers."

I sensed a Teachable Moment.

"First, let's have a round of applause for the students who entered this race because they really, really care about the school," said Kulbarsh.

I sank low in my seat.

"But only one of you can win. Only <u>one</u> person can preside over student council meetings, supervise committees, and serve as a liaison to the school board."

Way to rub it in!

"Keep the loss in perspective," Kulbarsh went on. "It's not the end of the world. Life will go on!"

"If only I could believe that," I whispered to Jasper, checking my watch. I weighed my defeat-party options: Burger Freak or Taco Dog?

"Announce it already!" someone yelled.

"Ladies and gentlemen, please welcome the new seventh-grade class president . . ." Kulbarsh tore open the envelope. He squinted at it hard and swallowed.

"Danny Shine."

* CHAPTER SIX *

No!

No!

No!

My stomach sank like a stone. Jasper gave me a push, and I stumbled up to the podium. People chanted, "Dan-ny! Dan-ny! Dan-ny!" Chantal stood up and cheered. I shook hands with Kulbarsh, staring up into his nostrils.

"You may address the class." Kulbarsh adjusted the mike. "But keep it under ten minutes."

TEN MINUTES????!!!!!

Sweat poured off my neck. This was a total freakin' nightmare.

"Umphg." The things rolling around inside my head weren't speech material.

It was like a dream where you scream and no words come out.

"Say something," Kulbarsh whispered.

I tried again. "Th-thanks for, uh, you know . . ."

After a few minutes of that, Kulbarsh walked me offstage. "Don't worry about freezing up there." He patted my back. "You'll be making other speeches."

I shuddered.

"Hundreds of them." He smiled.

"Where did we go wrong?" I moaned.

Jasper and I shook our heads, bewildered. We should have been at Burger Freak celebrating my defeat. Instead, we were slumped on the school steps while I waited to meet the outgoing president, Dex St. John.

"I don't get it." Jasper rubbed his forehead. "We put together the worst campaign of all time. Your platform was insane. Your slogans sucked. Your video reeked." He sighed. "What happened?"

We shook our heads, but we both knew who was to blame.

"Chantal," I burst out.

"Man." Jasper shook his head. "How powerful _is_ she anyway?"

I shrugged. "How powerful was Mussolini?"

CHANTAL

People began pouring out of school. I didn't want them to see me. I pulled up my hoodie, furious at myself. Why did I ever go to that stupid info meeting? Getting mangled by Bruiser would have taken twenty minutes. Being president was for THE WHOLE YEAR.

A whole year. Of sweating over speeches, endless meetings, and debates over recycling rules.

What an idiot I'd been.

"Presi-dude," someone called out.

"Congratulations, Danny!" sang Sophie.

I tried to smile and nod. Then I felt an arm around my neck, and suddenly I was gasping for air.

"Ah! Ah!" I couldn't breathe.

"'S just me." Axl let go and slumped down next to me. That was his way of saying hello. I took deep gulps of air.

"I can't believe you won." Axl shook his head. "Freakin' Chantal."

"Yeah. Well." I felt awkward. "Sorry about —"

"Naaaah." Axl waved his hand. "I couldn't really do the president thing _and_ be head of the Skulls. They're both, like, pretty major jobs."

"Right." I tried to imagine a tough day at the office for Axl.

He gave me a parting arm-twist and left. I looked around for Dex, feeling more and more depressed. Jasper saw me brooding and sighed, impatiently.

"Look, Danny." Jasper's voice rose. "You won. SO WHAT? It's not the end of the world."

"I guess."

"It's not like you puked in public, or caught a flesh-eating virus."

"Right."

"You'll still play Garage Band and read Rat Girl and get beaten by me at Halo."

"Yeah."

"So cheer up." Jasper stood up, ending the conversation. "Losing isn't everything."

*   *   *

"You know what the best part of the job is?"

Dex St. John strolled down the hall with lazy-jock confidence. As our outgoing class president, he was showing me the ropes. He was a good-looking Cool Table regular in a football jacket, usually surrounded by girls, so this was our first conversation, ever. He stopped suddenly.

"Your own key to the Media Room." He opened the door. "Check the score of a game whenever you want."

"Great." I tried to sound excited.

"See the prop closet?" His eyes gleamed. "You can bring girls here. Totally private."

"Oh. Good." Like I'd be doing that a lot.

"There's more too." Dex brought me over to

the student council office.
"Here are hall passes.
Now you're a free man.
Burger Freak, Funland,
or the go-kart track?
The choice is yours."

   "Wow." This was a surprise. I thought I'd be
getting a book of rules and a lecture about
respecting the faculty.

   "And here's the sweetest thing." He took
a metal box out of a locked cabinet. "Petty
cash. Write down all expenses in this ledger. Like
when you _really, really_ need chili cheese curly
fries."

   I gulped. Did that mean he "borrowed"
money and replaced it later? Being trusted with
a boxful of cash was wild. No wonder people
wanted to be president. I was starting to see
the job in a new light.

"You can also get rides," Dex continued.
"The school district has a driver who'll take you
places if you ask. Make it seem legit, like the
library. Once he drops you off? Boom! You hit
the Nike store."

Dex's lecture should have been called Gaming
the System. Why had I dreaded it? He almost
made the job sound appealing. I thought
presidents were earnest do-gooders, or wonky

student councilites. But Dex barely mentioned "work" at all.

"This job can't be just rides and free passes," I said. "It's a lot of work too. Right?"

He looked up from his phone. "What?"

"There's a lot of meetings. And committees. And speeches." I gripped the cash box. "Aren't there?"

Dex leaned over. "I'll let you in on a little secret."

I blinked.

"IT'S A BREEZE."

"What???" My eyes widened. "Really?"

"God, yes." He waved his hand. "Hardly anyone comes to meetings. A bunch of girls run everything — all you have to do is say, 'Sounds fine.' Do you care if the Valentine's dance has pink balloons or red?"

I shook my head.

"Neither do I. So you let _them_ do it." He leaned back on a swivel chair. "And you enjoy the good life."

Wow.

"You really didn't give speeches?" I stammered.

"Once I introduced someone at a meeting," Dex shrugged. "Another time I read cafeteria rules over the PA. It wasn't the Gettysburg Address."

"But —" This couldn't be right. "A lot of people showed up at the election info session."

Dex took a Jolly Rancher out and unwrapped it. "Everyone wants to run for president. But when the election's over, they lose interest."

"Why did you run?" I asked.

He moved the candy from cheek to cheek. Finally, he spit it out.

"To impress some girl?" For the first time, he sounded unsure of himself. "Do something my brother hasn't done? I don't remember. Probably, I just liked how it sounded: Class President. Stupid, huh?"

Hmmm. Maybe no one had good reasons for doing anything. We were all just flailing around, trying to do what felt least wrong.

"Hey." Dex looked at his watch. "I've got to

haul butt to football practice. Being president rocks. As long as you never, ever, ever do one thing..."

I leaned forward. "What's that?"

"Decide anything major," he said.

Okay. Whatever.

"I'm not triflin', bro." His voice was low. "Don't put yourself in a position where you can be blamed."

I scratched my chin. "Isn't deciding stuff my job?"

"No!" Dex locked eyes with me. "Your job is keeping your job. Let other people take the heat. You've got more to lose."

"But —" This was confusing. "What happens when people disagree?"

"Then you appoint a committee." Dex waved his hand. "To 'research' it. Kick the can down the road. That way, the issue gets put off till the next meeting — or better yet — forgotten about."

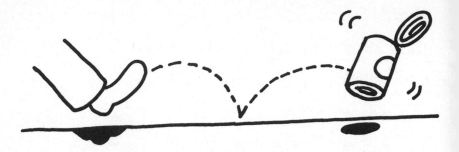

"Later, man." He picked up a gym bag and winked. "Don't hog the prop closet!"

"I'll try not to." Weak smile.

"Hey, Danny!"

As I flew down the school steps, Asia grabbed me.

"You!" Her eyes were shining. "You won! You pulled it off! Even after all that nonsense about dress codes. Wow."

"Oh. Yeah." My neck got warm. "I was just —"

"This is so great!" She squealed.

It was?

"Now we can work on what we talked about!" she said. I looked at her blankly. "Real stuff! Not 'Should the bake sale cookies have chocolate chips or Reese's Pieces?'"

"Um, yeah, totally," I stammered.

"We need time together." Her eyebrows knitted. "Plan a strategy."

"Yeah. Yes!" I nodded my head up and down vigorously. _Asia O'Neill — suggesting a get-together!_ _Where would we go?_

"How about the Multi-Purpose Room?" she asked.

"Okay." I tried not to sound deflated.

She inched closer. The cherry-Twizzler smell of her hair was stronger than ever.

"We're going to do great things," she said. "Walk me to African drumming."

I happily obeyed, thinking once again:

Maybe this job won't be so bad after all.

* CHAPTER SEVEN *

School
Participation
Interest
Respect
Integrity
Teamwork

"Is this Fashion Club?" Angie Bilandic peeked inside the classroom.

"Student council," I said.

"Oops! Sorry!" Angie and her friend burst into giggles and fled.

Malibu Nussbaum and I exchanged looks. So far, she and I were the only ones in the Multi-Purpose Room. Maybe Dex was right: This would be easy. As the first runner-up, Malibu had been

made vice president. She congratulated me
and made a peace offering.

"Take some," she ordered. "These meetings
go on forever."

We waited for more people. Soon, Ginnifer
Baxter and Katelyn Ogleby sat down. Pinky
Shroeder, inexplicably. The kid with wild dark
hair always writing in his notebook. Kendra
Maxtone-Cousins came by, saying she had a
half hour before competitive figure skating.
Which brought the grand total to . . .

Seven.

Luckily, we only had three agenda items.

I could be home by four thirty, I realized happily. I was at a crucial moment in drawing my new e-comic, The Thing That Ate Winnetka, and couldn't wait to get back to it. Hopefully the meeting would fly by.

"Ty will be late," Kendra announced flatly. "He's collecting blankets for animal shelters."

Of course.

"Let's get started." I swallowed and looked at my clipboard. "As you know, I'm the new, uh, student council president." I looked up uncertainly, anticipating their reaction.

"First on the agenda is . . . let me just find it . . ." I started.

"Announcements!" Ginnifer interrupted impatiently. "Announcements are always first." She nudged Katelyn, like she couldn't believe my cluelessness.

"Oh, okay." I rubbed my forehead. Fumbling through my notes, I found something to announce.

"The school Lost and Found has an unclaimed tube sock," I said.

Silence.

"Now it's the secretary's turn." Ginnifer nodded at Katelyn.

Katelyn opened her spiral notebook. "I will now read minutes from the last meeting. Progress was made on three agenda items." She lifted her chin. "We decided Woodchuck Pride bumper stickers should be in school colors."

Wasn't that kind of a no-brainer?

"And the basketball contest will be held in the gym."

Ditto.

"And pierced belly buttons aren't allowed with formal dresses," she finished.

Everyone pondered that.

"Thanks, Katelyn. Next up . . ." I checked my clipboard. "Menu for the Wild West Barbecue."

"Pigs in blankets," said Ginnifer and Katelyn at the same time.

"Let's do something healthier," Malibu said. "Tacos with tomatoes and avocado slices."

"Sounds great." I was always pro-taco.

"How about cultural diversity?" Kendra said. "Pad Thai. Samosas."

"For a barbecue!?" Katelyn snorted. "That's dumb."

Kendra stood up. "Who says?"

"Everyone says!" Katelyn looked around, trying to drum up support.

The two faced each other.

We heard a noise at the door. It was Ty, with his hair all swept around his face. "Sorry I'm late."

"We were just talking about the Wild West Barbecue menu," I said. "Pigs in blankets, healthy tacos, samosas —"

"Samosas! Cool!" Ty said.

"That's <u>whacked</u>," Ginnifer wailed. "Barbecues don't have exotic food!"

"Okay, let's take this up later," I said, trying to switch the topic to something less controversial. "How about . . . fund-raising?"

"We could have a student store that sells pencils and notebooks," suggested Malibu.

"A craft fair is better." Katelyn's voice rose. "With friendship bracelets and spice racks and dressed-up teddy bears."

That sounded scary.

"Sing-o-grams!" yelled Ginnifer.

"Dog-walking!"

"Bikini car wash!"

"Good suggestions." I remembered Dex's advice. "Why don't we have a committee to research it?" Ginnifer and Malibu raised their hands eagerly. "Okay. Done," I said, relieved.

"We should check the student suggestion box," said Malibu, holding it up. "Feels pretty full."

She handed me a dented shoe box with "You suck" scrawled on the side. "Look," Malibu said, pointing to the graffiti. "Time for a new one. Again."

I stuck my hand through the slot. "Here goes nothing." A strange smell came from inside. And why did something in there feel wet?

I pulled out a Snickers wrapper, a broken barrette, and a peach pit. Finally, my hand connected to a slip of paper. I unfolded it.

"Kiss my booty," I read aloud.

Everyone laughed.

"Can I read one?" Ginnifer pulled out another slip of paper, looked at it, and then folded it up. "Sorry," she said. "I'm not allowed to say that word."

"Obviously, we need a new box," said Katelyn. "The only people who put suggestions in are psychos. I've got one from Shoe Barn. I could decorate it with stickers and puff paint. Neon pink so you can't miss it."

"Not pink!" Kendra gagged.

"How about brown?" asked Pinky.

"NOT BROWN!!" gasped Ginnifer and Katelyn.

My head was about to explode. Were we really fighting over what color to paint the suggestion box?

"We'll continue this another time," I said. "Next topic —"

"No!" Malibu said. "That's why these meetings go on forever! Just decide."

I frowned. "But Dex said —"

"Dex!" Malibu spat out his name. "That guy was totally checked out. All he did was play Nerf basketball and high-five people."

The disgust in her voice made me ashamed. I'd been hungry for Dex's tips on how to cut corners, resolving not to let student council ruin my life. But now I found myself — strangely — not wanting to disappoint Malibu.

　"You don't want to be that kind of president." Malibu shook her head.

　Maybe not. But what kind did I want to be?

　"Okay." I rubbed my hands together. "Katelyn, you take over. Make it any color but pink. Try to have it by the next meeting."

　"Sure." Katelyn looked pleased.

　It only took another <u>hour</u> to decide rules for Pajama Day. The final results:

　Slipper-socks allowed.

Okay to bring stuffed animals.

No boxer shorts!

WHEW! We didn't finish up until four thirty. Malibu and I walked out together.

"Does it always take this long to resolve this little?" I asked her. "What if we had something really big to decide?"

Malibu waved her hand. "Never happens. We've been sidelined at this school. The student council doesn't matter. So we've never really had to come together."

"Huh."

"There's lots of room for improvement," she said. "You could take that as a challenge."

I thought about how Dex was both right and wrong. The job was easy to blow off. But if you took it seriously, it would be hard. Really hard.

Luckily, I didn't have to.

Waving good-bye to Malibu, I hurried off. I had mutilated zombies to draw.

* CHAPTER EIGHT *

"THREE THOUSAND DOLLARS?" I gasped. "Really?"

I was sitting in the principal's office, next to Kulbarsh. Across from me sat a heavyset, red-faced man in a giant hat.

"I'm sorry." I blinked. "Who . . . who _are_ you, again?"

"Bill Banacek." He leaned over to shake my hand. "Royal Order of Porcupines."

Minutes before, Mrs. Lacewell had gotten me out of class, saying, "The principal wants you to meet someone." She made me tuck in my shirt and wipe mustard off my arm.

When we got to the principal's office, Kulbarsh explained, "Mr. Banacek here wants to make a very generous gift to Gerald Ford."

Now Banacek was showing me a check.

"This — this is great," I stammered.

"It's part of our Three Cheers for Middle School program," Banacek said. "Help kids do something besides destroy their brains with violent video games and mind-rotting television."

"Oh."

"I hope you can help," he said.

"Sure." I nodded. Right after I play Gangsta's Revenge and watch World's Worst Car Wrecks.

Kulbarsh leaned forward. "What Mr. Banacek is saying is, the school needs to come up with a plan on how to spend the money. Which is a wonderful project for the student council."

"The student council?" I gulped.

"Of course."

"But —" we nearly came to blows over whether the student suggestion box should have stickers on it! "Shouldn't this be decided by some responsible adult?"

"Horse manure!" Banacek banged his fist on the desk. "This is _for_ kids, so _they_ should decide. Within reason, of course. We're not handing over three Gs to blow at the dog track."

"Yes, of course," Kulbarsh said smoothly. "The student council will get right on it. Danny is the new president, and he'll lead the way. Next week we'll have the special assembly, where you will officially hand him the check. That's when he'll announce how the money will be spent."

One week! My head started to throb. Meetings were only twice a month, and it took a whole one just to decide no boxer shorts for Pajama Day.

After Banacek left, Kulbarsh turned to his computer. I had to at least _try_ to explain how dysfunctional the student council was. I stood in front of his desk and fidgeted with a heavy glass paperweight decorated with the school logo.

"Um, sir." I cleared my throat. "I know you want this decision to be made by us. But are you sure you want the student council on this? People have a really hard time, you know, agreeing on —"

"Danny," Kulbarsh interrupted. "Have you ever been to a PTA meeting?"

"Uh, no, sir."

"Sheer bedlam." He turned to me. "People disagree on everything: The number of recycling bins! Whether to continue Spanish language immersion! When to schedule Pizza Bingo! If the coffee should be decaf!"

"Wow, sir," I said. "That must be —"

"Torture." Kulbarsh's face was flushed. "Everyone has a complaint. Parents of gifted students, early growers, poor spellers, non-meat eaters, slow readers, high jumpers, kids who have peanut allergies, advanced math skills, or two dads."

"I hear you," I said, but he was just getting started.

"The crosswalk needs repainting!" He was standing up now. "The school musical doesn't have enough roles! Passing periods are too short! Tests are too hard! Gym suits too itchy!"

I got the picture. Parents were an even bigger pain in the butt than their kids.

"When I was younger," Kulbarsh said in a low voice, "I'd give myself pep talks in the mirror before meetings."

"Huh. Wow." Was this the same stone-faced enforcer I knew?

"You can do it, I'd say," he went on. "You're the principal! People are scared of you!"

"Gosh." This was getting weird.

Then suddenly, Kulbarsh bolted up straight, as if remembering who he was. "But that was when I was younger." He sat down at his desk, ending the meeting. "Much, much younger."

I nodded again.

"Call an emergency meeting." He turned back to his computer. "You don't have much time."

"WOO-HOO!!!!" Jasper whooped.

His excitement took me by surprise. Banacek's gift had struck me as a problem, not cause for celebrating. But when I told Jasper at Burger Freak, he almost spit out his soda.

"Oh yeah. Oh yeah. Oh yeah." Jasper did a happy dance in his seat.

I dragged a french fry through a pool of ketchup.

"You're not excited." He stopped dancing. "Why?"

I shrugged.

"This is the answer to our problems!" He spread his arms. "We can finally make our monster truck zombie movie."

I nearly choked on a fry.

"What — WHAT?" I sputtered. "It's not up to me. It's up to the student council!"

"Ye-ah." Jasper smiled. "And who runs the student council?"

"No. No!" I shook my head. "I can't just do what I want! The group decides."

"I got you." Jasper nodded. "Infiltrate the system, then — subvert it."

"Jasper." I lowered my voice. "I wish it was my call, but it's not. Believe me, I could think of plenty ways to spend it."

"Spend what?" Phil Petrokis crammed into our booth. Ahmet Sayid piled in too. Jasper and I slid over to make room.

"Three thousand mithril." Jasper smiled.

Phil whistled.

"They're about to announce it," I said. "Some group — the Royal Brotherhood of Weasels? The Loyal Order of Groundhogs? — wants to give the school money so we won't play video games."

"Good luck with <u>that</u>." Ahmet snorted.

"Point <u>is</u>," Jasper said, "the student council gets to spend it. Normally, that would leave us out cold. But Danny's president, so . . . start working on your zombie makeup."

Phil and Ahmet stared. "You mean . . . ?"

Jasper nodded. "Mutant Truckers from Planet Gorbleck lives. Even if the zombies don't."

"YES!" Phil and Ahmet high-fived.

"Jasper's delusional," I moaned. "It's up to the <u>student council</u>! Like they're not going to want it for something dumb."

"But the whole school can be involved!" Phil burst out. "We'll need an army of zombie truck drivers. Those cars aren't going to crush themselves!"

"We can use food coloring for fake blood," said Ahmet.

"Ground beef for mutilated flesh —"

"Plaster casts for severed limbs!"

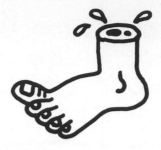

"Don't get your hopes up," I said. "Seriously."

But they didn't hear me. There was too much to discuss — how Ahmet could borrow his father's video camera, and Jasper could learn Final Cut Pro to edit with.

"Danny could do storyboards," Jasper said, and suddenly my skin started to tingle too.

Then I joined in with my own ideas for jazzy camera angles and special effects. Why not shoot a school zombie movie? The project wasn't just cool — it was educational. It could involve everyone. My heart started to race.

Maybe getting our way wasn't so far-fetched. I was president, right? It was time to act like one.

* CHAPTER NINE *

Everyone in the Multi-Purpose Room was shouting. Malibu and I looked at each other, overwhelmed. Today there had to be seventy-five people here, at least! Visitors were always allowed, but usually no one showed up. We looked helplessly at our adviser, Mr. Amundson, but he just stood there checking his phone.

"You'd think it was a party at Angie Bilandic's," said Malibu.

I laughed and unstacked more chairs. The

size of the crowd shouldn't have surprised us after the principal's PA announcement.

"The school is receiving a three-thousand-dollar gift," he'd said. "If you want to decide how to spend it, come to the student council meeting after school."

Every kind of person was there.

Jocks   Geeks   Cool Tablers   Girly girls   Serious girls

Skaters   Haters   Chantal-ites   Goof-offs   Spelling freaks

"Danny! Over here!" shouted Jasper. I shook my head, wishing I were standing with him, Phil, and Ahmet. Unfortunately, Malibu and I had to stay up front to run the meeting. Even the Skulls — Axl, Boris, and Spike — were here, circling around some nervous-looking sixth graders. And then I saw a familiar curtain of black hair.

I swallowed. It was Asia, looking excellent in an oversize red bowling shirt with NORM sewn on the pocket. She was sitting yoga-style in a folding chair, reading a Shadow Grrrl comic.

Could she be any cooler?

"DANNY!" Chantal shouted. "WHAT'S UP WITH THE THREE GRAND?"

The noise stopped.

"So we got this money," I began. "And we — the student council — get to decide how to spend it. Let's hear your ideas."

Everyone started yelling.

"Cubs game!" "Bears game!" "Fashion show!"

"Hey, people? One at a time!" Amundson shouted.

"We should have an _American Idol_-type competition," Chantal pleaded.

Axl popped up. "That's lame. What this school needs is a Battle of the Bands. Fight it out with guitars and tear this sucker _down_." No doubt he pictured Mutilator — his band — soaring to glory in a sea of pumping fists.

"That reeks," announced Tank Friedman, a beefy jock who looked incomplete without a giant foam #1 hand. "What we need is a —"

"PAINTBALL WAR!!!!!" boomed the jock corner.

"School-wide. All day. Wilson Field," Tank said.

Huge guys with weapons. Great.

"Paintball! Paintball! Paintball!" the jocks chanted.

This was getting out of hand. Where were Phil, Jasper, and Ahmet, so we could pitch our brilliant idea? I saw them in the crowd and waved my hand furiously. "Get up here!" I mouthed.

Phil rushed forward. He was the slickest of the tech geeks, and the best one to sell it. Go, Phil!

"Hey, everybody! Who wants to be in a zombie movie?" he asked the crowd.

A few people raised their hands.

"Would I be totally rotted?" asked Pinky Shroeder. "Or still have brain activity?"

"You've barely got it _now_," Chantal said.

"Up to you." Phil held up a poster. "_Mutant Truckers from Planet Gorbleck_ has a role for everyone. It's got it all..."

"Decapitation."

"Severed limbs."

"Monster trucks."

"Eeew!" said the girls.

"Cool!" said the guys.

The red bowling shirt quietly moved to the front of the room. I watched Asia waiting to speak, grateful for the chance to stare at her.

"Um, Asia, did you have an idea?" I asked.

She turned to the crowd and held up a paper bird. "There's an ancient Japanese legend. Anyone who folds a thousand origami cranes is granted good luck. If every student here made one, we could decorate the children's hospital and fill their courtyard with beautiful plants."

Ty came forward. "A Thousand Cranes sounds awesome."

He and Asia locked eyes across the room.

"Great idea! I agree! Totally!" I sputtered, desperate to break the Ty-Asia mind-meld.

"Danny," Jasper reminded me. "You're for the zombie movie."

Yeah, but —

Asia's long black hair fanned out like a paintbrush, and I felt myself wavering. Now she was putting a strand in her mouth —

Crud!

"Is there anyone else?" I asked. The guy with the wild dark hair stood up and shut his notebook.

"My name's Dinesh. I'm new here, and" — he took a deep breath — "I wrote a Bollywood musical."

"What's Bollywood?" someone asked.

Dinesh swallowed. "It's a kind of movie from India that's really over the top. With big, crazy production numbers."

"What's it called?" I asked.

"The Highest Score. About thieves who steal the SAT answers." He pulled a thick script out of his messenger bag.

"Can I see?" I asked.

"Sure," he said, handing it to me. "Took me two years, working lunch and after school." You could hear pride in his voice.

I thumbed through it. The first song, "Vocabulary Flash Card Blues," featured a chorus line of test-prep tutors. Another scene had dancing number-two pencils. It looked pretty funny.

"You wrote the songs?" I asked, jealous.

He nodded.

Wow. Our zombie script was a direct rip-off of a famous fifties horror movie. But this guy had written an original musical with more than a dozen songs. I was impressed.

"Let me see!" Chantal demanded.

"Who is he?" Katelyn asked.

"Maybe we should do this one," I blurted out.

"WHAT?" The whole room gasped.

"It seems... funny and original, just the kind of student show we should put on," I said. Seeing all the anxious faces, I toned it down. "But of course, we've heard lots of great ideas..."

"Battle of the Bands!"

"Zombies!"

"PAINT<u>BALL</u>! PAINT<u>BALL</u>! PAINT<u>BALL</u>!"

It was time for the big vote. Counting all the raised hands was an ordeal. And the winner was...

A three-way tie.

<u>Crud</u>! It was between paintball, <u>Idol</u>, and the Snowflake Dance. We voted two more times — same result. Finally, the third time, Kirby Hammer shifted his vote to paintball. The deadlock was broken.

Finally!

"And the winner is... Paintball-a-Palooza."

The jocks exploded into cheers and chest bumps. I'd been hoping either our zombie movie or the cool original musical would win. I gave Jasper a "what can you do?" shrug. At our school, jocks ruled. Asia's shoulders sagged under her bowling shirt, and I mouthed, "I'm sorry."

But in a way...?

I was relieved. Now I could go back to comic book drawing, and the student council could go back to debating the color of the student suggestion box. None of us was up to this.

"Danny?" Ginnifer came up, waving a pamphlet. I couldn't hear her over the noise.

"Woo-hoo! PAINTBALL!" yelled the jocks.

She pulled me aside. "The by-laws say any spending decision has to have a two-thirds majority for spending initiatives. So paintball didn't win!"

"What?" I grabbed the pamphlet.

The jocks got wilder. "You're going to get HOSED, Vandershaf!"

Amundson looked over my shoulder. "She's right."

What a stupid rule!

Now what was I supposed to do? Tell ten huge guys they were out of luck? That their paintball dream wasn't happening? What would they do to me?

I went back to the front of the room and cleared my throat.

"Um . . . guys?"

The celebration continued.

"Heads up!"

No reaction.

"PAINTBALL DIDN'T WIN!" I shouted.

That finally got their attention.

"Turns out we need a two-thirds majority."
My heart was pounding. "I'm really sorry."

"NOOOOOOOOOOOOOOOOOOOOOOOOOO!"
thundered the jock
corner.

"We won!" Tank's
face was red.
"You said!"

"PAINTBALL! PAINTBALL! PAINTBALL!"

"People, yo!" Amundson fluttered his hands.
"Be cool!"

"He got our hopes up!" Tank pointed at me.
He looked at his fellow jocks. "Don't just sit
there. GET HIM!"

The jocks sprang up. I leaped for the door just as the whole pack of them lunged.

"FIGHT!" Everyone yelled.

I bolted for the door, making it halfway out. Tank grabbed my legs, trying to drag me back. Frantically, I gripped the door frame as my stomach hit the floor. As Tank pulled, my pants slid down a few inches, and suddenly, I felt cold air on my skin.

"OHHHH!" The room gasped. Tank looked stunned.

Holy crud!

They were staring at my naked butt.

* CHAPTER TEN *

"BARE BUTT!"

"BARE BUTT!"

I came to school the next day expecting to hear those words over and over. But when I saw Chantal, she just nodded and said, "Hi." A few minutes later, I ran into Axl, who gave me a friendly smile! No embarrassing nickname, no graffiti on my locker.

Something was definitely wrong.

Then Tank came up to me in the hall, and my chest started to pound. Here it comes.

But he merely looked at the floor.

"Sorry about, uh . . ." He coughed. "You know."

HUH?

"When I grabbed you, I wasn't trying to —" He bit his fingernail. "I swear! All of a sudden, your pants were, like, down . . . but we were just mad about not winning! I didn't mean it!"

I listened, amazed. What new universe was this, where bullies apologized for "not meaning it"?

"'S okay." I shrugged.

"So." He took a deep breath. "Do you want to, uh, get some lunch?"

GET SOME LUNCH?

This was getting weirder and weirder. The day before he'd mauled me, and now he wanted lunch? I felt disoriented, but — it couldn't hurt to walk to the cafeteria together. "Okay."

Inside, he steered me to the Jock Table. The four biggest guys from our class were already sitting down. They greeted one another with high fives.

"Dan-ny!" Kyle Larson gave me a fake karate chop.

No one seemed surprised to see me. Bruiser Pekarsky, the muscle-bound wrestler, slid over to make room. "Abs" Tanaka, the super-fit soccer player, threw me a sandwich.

"Sit," commanded Kyle, his mouth full of food.

    <u>Should I?</u> I looked longingly at the Tech Geek table. They'd be talking about the new Apple store, or the Hulk versus the Blob, or who was the worst James Bond villain. I tried to catch Jasper's eye. How would I explain?

    But I sat down.

    Tearing open the sandwich foil, I was happy to find a hot meatball sub from the Beast, a food truck across the street. I bit into it hungrily. <u>Not bad!</u> Tank pointed to the spread.

"Pekarsky sneaks out during third period," he said. "So we eat like kings."

Sure enough, the table was a junk-food lover's dream.

"So — um — Danny." Tank cleared his throat. "About our paintball idea —"

"Back off, Friedman," Vandershaf warned. "Guy wants to eat. At the game, we'll have time to talk."

Game? What game?

Vandershaf drained a jumbo soda. "We're taking you to the Raptors playoffs Saturday. In Oak Glen. Should be awesome." They were our high school's football team.

"If this is about selling me on paintball —" I put down my sandwich. "You're wasting your time. Because it's not my call — it's up to the student council."

The guys looked at one another. "Didn't anyone tell you?" asked Kyle.

I shook my head.

"After you left the meeting, Amundson announced if the student council couldn't reach a two-thirds majority, the president gets to decide how to spend the money."

My jaw dropped.

"So it's up to _me_?" I gasped. "Are you _sure_?"

The jocks nodded.

Holy crud.

My head started to throb. Amundson, where was Amundson? He could confirm this. Scanning the room, I saw him near the entrance. "I'll be back," I said to the jocks, and then bolted toward the assistant principal, almost knocking him over.

"Ow." Amundson rubbed his elbow.

"Sorry." I was out of breath. "Is it true?"

"It's in the bylaws, page four." Amundson nodded. "'In the event

of gridlock,' it says. The school founders anticipated this! Pretty fly, huh?"

"Huh. I guess."

"You da' man." Amundson fist-bumped me.

I started back toward the jocks, in a daze. After a few steps, someone tugged at my sleeve. "Hey, Danny." It was Angie Bilandic, wearing thick eye makeup, as usual. Had she ever spoken to me directly?

"Party this weekend," she whispered. "I'll text you."

Text me? Did she even know my —

"Danny!" It was Raina, Chantal's friend. "Come to our table." Dragging me by my shirt, she yelled, "Da'Nise! Move that purse over!"

"I can't, I'm already sitting with —" I started, but even more people crowded around.

"Danny! Sit with us!"

"Over here, SHINE!"

"DAAAAAAAAANNNNNNNNNNNNY!!!"

Overnight, I'd become the cafeteria's Most Wanted Lunch Partner. People who barely knew my name now fought to sit next to me. At first, they were amazingly friendly, offering to share food, gossip, and test answers. Then they moved in for the kill.

"So here's why you should choose the Snowflake Dance," said Ginnifer, tearing open another bag of candy. "Kit Kat bar?"

"Mphlfhm." My mouth was already full of Swedish Fish.

All week I got offers to play Garage Band, go skateboarding, or hang out in front of 7-Eleven. People walked with me down the hall and laughed at my jokes. I wasn't used to the royal treatment.

"You're never around," complained Jasper.

"It's this stupid job." I shoveled more gourmet jelly beans into my mouth.

I missed Jasper and the guys, but it was fun to hear a chorus of "Hey, Dannys" in the cafeteria and have a choice of where to sit. The jocks were even sort of friendly, and girls talked to me. So what if they were just sucking up to sell their idea for a rock-climbing wall or scrapbooking cruise? I liked the attention and free food.

There was just one little problem:

I couldn't say no.

Like when Axl tried to sell me on Battle of the Bands. He and Boris and Spike took me to Funland, where they planted me in front of a machine and kept pumping in quarters. While I played, Axl went into his pitch.

"We need to decide who rules the school," he said. "Band-wise."

"Uh-huh." I zapped another shark.

"Is Mutilator better?" Axl's voice rose dramatically. "Or the Terrible Turds?" Like it was the world's most burning question.

"Hmmm."

"You agree, right?" He got in my face.

"I'm not sure." I shifted my weight to my other foot. "I don't know if there are enough bands at school to have a real battle..."

Axl looked stunned.

"ENOUGH BANDS?" Axl roared. "ENOUGH BANDS!?"

Oh, boy.

"How about Dangerwolf?" he exploded. "Pus Train? Kiki's Mascara?"

He started stomping around and muttering, "Gimme a freakin' break!"

I ran for the door, but Boris and Spike grabbed me. Dragging me into the corner, they made their best argument.

"Okay! Okay!" I gasped. "I'll work on it!"

"Let me at him." Axl came over.

Still red-faced, he twisted my arm until I cried out. "You'll go to bat for us, right?" Axl twisted it more. "RIGHT?"

"Right," I choked out.

*　　　*　　　*

By the end of the week, I could barely walk to class without being assaulted.

"Glad you're on the paintball train, bro..." Tank gave me a fake right hook.

"I never said I was —"

"DUDE!!!" His buddies came over and blasted me with high fives.

Dinesh walked by. "My dad wants you to have this bookmark, Danny." He gave me a piece of cloth strip with gold lettering on it. "As thanks. For getting my musical put on."

My chest sank. "But, Dinesh! I haven't decided —" He just waved and disappeared into the crowd.

"Hey, Danny! Wait up!" Chantal waved. "I've got another idea for Middle School Idol!"

I pulled up my sweatshirt hood and ran away, my head throbbing. They were coming after me like a swarm of bees!

Tap-tap.

I felt something on my arm and spun around. It was Asia. My stomach dropped, and my pulse raced.

"Hey, Danny."

Even in my agitated state, I took in the long hair, the messenger bag, the ACME EXTERMINATION

T-shirt. The cherry-Twizzler smell. She took something out of her bag pocket, and pressed it into my fingers. I held the piece of paper, dampened by her hand.

"It's a crane," she said.

Her charity project! My chest tightened again.

"No!" I tried to hand it back. "You shouldn't give it to me! I can't promise —"

"Shhhh." She pressed it toward me. "Don't talk. Just look."

I stared at the creases in the paper, amazed at how it suggested a bird in a few simple shapes. The wings even flapped. Holding something she had made was strangely powerful.

"Hmm," I said quietly.

"Yeah." She cupped her hands over it, like a real bird.

I stayed silent for a bit. For a moment, it seemed like we were on a beach somewhere, not in front of a row of lockers at Gerald Ford Middle School.

"Now picture a thousand of them." She lifted her arms.

I looked up at the imaginary flock and then back at her. Had her breath stopped too?

Our eyes locked.

"We can make this happen." Her voice was low.

Keep it going — don't ruin it.

"We will. Absolutely," I heard myself saying.

She made the bird flap its wings a few times.

"Hearing you say that," she said, "makes me really happy."

By then, I was past the point of no return. I would have said yes to anything.

<u>Holy freakin' crud!</u>

Escaping school that day, my heart beat like crazy. I bolted out the side entrance to avoid hearing, "Danny! DANNY!" All day I'd been counting the minutes until I'd be at Burger Freak with Jasper, Phil, and Ahmet.

What a relief it would be to snarf down fries and tell them all the crazy stuff that happened. How the jocks tried to drag me to a football game, and how Axl nearly beat me up. How everyone thought I owed them. How if I heard one more pitch, I was going to barf.

"Greetings and salutations," Jasper called from the corner booth. A plate of fries was already on the table.

"Yo." Ahmet fake-belched.

Phil pelted me with a wadded-up permission slip.

It was good to be back.

"What's going on?" Jasper asked. "It's like suddenly you're the pope, or mayor, or CEO of Apple."

I leaned over, anxious to unload. "Everyone's breathing down my neck. They all think they should get their way: 'You better pick Battle of the Bands!' 'Middle School Idol — or else!' But there are a million groups, and I can only pick one. It sucks."

"Oh, man."

"What a drag."

"Geez."

Their sympathetic groans made me feel better. Looking around the table, I felt grateful. I'd missed them.

"Sounds like torture." Jasper shook his head.

"Yeah," said Phil. "Don't they know you've already decided?"

My stomach dropped.

"On what?" I asked.

"The zombie movie!" Phil burst out.

Oh, crud.

I looked around the table. Jasper, Phil, and Ahmet were all looking at me expectantly.

"We thought it was a done deal," said Jasper. "You had to look like you were giving everyone a chance. But we knew you'd pick the zombie movie. How could you _not_? You helped write it."

My head felt like it was about to burst. They were just as bad as everyone else. Didn't they understand?

"You didn't change your mind!" Ahmet's eyes narrowed. "Did you?"

"I don't know," I admitted.

"No!" "Come on!" "Seriously?"

"It's the _perfect_ group project!" Jasper was turning red. "You said! It has zombies, monster trucks, and giant aquatic millipedes!"

"But I'm president of everyone," I burst out. "Not just us."

They all looked at me.

"I have to figure out what other people want too," I said. "I don't want us to get our way if it makes ninety-nine percent of the school unhappy."

Jasper fixed his eyes on me.

"Ninety-nine percent of the school will be unhappy no matter who you pick," he said. "So you might as well pick us."

He had a point.

"Can't you just do this for me?" Jasper asked. After all I've done for you, he was probably thinking. And he did do stuff for me, every day.

* WHAT FRIENDS ARE FOR

To give compliments

To share things

To tell you the truth

To <u>not</u> tell you the truth

It wasn't about heroic acts or fancy gifts. The best thing someone could give you was their time. And he'd given me plenty.

"So are you in?" Phil lifted his chin.

"I'll, um, see what I can do..." I nodded.

"All <u>right</u>!" they shouted.

Then we all did the Rat Girl secret handshake, and I felt a tightness in my chest. Somehow, I had done it again.

* CHAPTER ELEVEN *

My life felt like a ticking time bomb.

The assembly was in three days, and I'd made promises to everyone. How could I possibly choose between:

My best friend

The world's coolest girl

My worst enemy

The super-powerful   The most talented   Everyone else

    The worst thing about it was not being able to talk to Jasper. Usually, he had really good advice. But in this case?

    He was part of the problem.

    "You're not choosing who you <u>like</u> most," Malibu reminded me as we stapled flyers in the student council office. "Or who you're most scared of. You're choosing what project would work best. For the school."

    I looked at her gratefully. At a time when things were weird with Jasper, I appreciated having someone to talk to. She seemed to view things from a wider angle. I had always dismissed her as a "student-council type," but she was — actually — pretty cool.

"I don't want to make everyone at school unhappy," I said.

"Oh, you will," she assured me.

"We could call another student council meeting," I said. "But could we get them to agree — on anything?"

* WHAT THE STUDENT COUNCIL MIGHT BE ABLE TO AGREE ON

Puppies are cute

Water is wet

Most people only have one nose

Malibu shook her head. "I don't see them coming together. You're not going to find a solution that pleases everyone. So just accept that, and bite the bullet."

Crud!

The rest of the day, I couldn't concentrate. As the deadline got closer, people still swarmed around me, but now their "Hey, Dannys" were more threatening.

"I saw you at Burger Freak with the zombie guys," Tank said in the hallway, wagging his finger. "You better not flake out on us!"

"Better not," drawled the other jocks.

Ginnifer put it more directly at lunch. "You ate our Skittles and drank our soda. Now you owe us."

Axl was even briefer. "No Battle of the Bands? No Danny."

How desperate <u>was</u> I?

Desperate enough to go to Kulbarsh. If he understood the bind I was in, maybe he'd take the decision off my hands. Sitting in the principal's office, I chewed on my pen, praying he could get me out of this.

"It's a disaster," I explained. "Everyone wants something <u>totally</u> different. And whatever I choose? I'm signing my own death warrant."

Kulbarsh leaned back in his chair and fixed his eyes on me.

"Danny." His voice was playful. "What would you like to do with the money?"

"Me?" I gulped.

"Forget everyone else." Kulbarsh waved his hand, as if shooing away a gnat. "In a perfect world, what would you do with it?"

Truthfully? I wasn't sure. At first, I was 100 percent behind the zombie movie. But Dinesh's proposal took me by surprise — it was such a cool project. Something in me wanted to reward his bravery — this new kid, writing a complete musical. Then I thought about Asia's paper bird. How could I turn her down when things between us might finally be going somewhere?

"I don't know," I admitted. "There are a few really good ideas. Could we split the money between projects?"

"No." Kulbarsh shook his head. "There's not enough to spread around."

Then take this off my hands, I begged silently. Find some unexciting but perfectly reasonable use for the money — more library books. Field trip to the aeronautical museum. New mats for gym class.

For a moment, we were both silent.

"Or . . . maybe I should take this over," Kulbarsh said casually, keeping his eyes on my face. "Sounds like this is too big a decision — for you or the student council."

Phew! Thank god!

"Okay," I said.

"Let's call the staff in, and see what they recommend," he said.

The staff? That sounded . . . worrisome.

Kulbarsh got on the intercom. "Mrs. Lacewell," he said. "I'd like Mr. Amundson, Mr. Brown, Mrs. Seafort, and yourself to come to my office. Thanks."

Just then, we had a knock on the door. It was my buddy Ralph, the part-time janitor/actor, with a squeegee in his hand, wheeling a bucket. "I'm just doing the windows," he announced. "I can come back later, if you want —"

"What I want, Ralph," Kulbarsh spun around to face him. "Is your opinion. What would you do with the three-thousand-dollar class gift?"

"LX-Turbomaster SL350." Ralph didn't blink. "AKA, 'The Maniac.'"

"What?" Kulbarsh cupped an ear.

"Vacuum cleaner." Ralph's eyes were dreamy. "State of the art. Sucks up vomit like nobody's business. Not to mention hardened gum wads. I'd give anything to give that baby a ride."

"Thank you, Ralph." Kulbarsh nodded. "Very helpful. You may go back to the windows."

In a moment, Lacewell appeared with Mr. Robinson, the security guard; Mrs. Seafort, the school nurse; and assistant principal Amundson.

"What would you do with a three-thousand-dollar class gift?" asked Kulbarsh.

   Good grief. These were the worst ideas EVER!

   "A security camera!" Kulbarsh banged his palm on the table. "That's the ticket! Put it in the lobby to track tardiness, or better yet, the stairwell . . ."

   The stairwell! That was a crucial epicenter of illicit student activity! It was where people

bought forged hall passes, got beat up, and
kissed.

Putting a security camera there would mean
we'd have NO place to get away. Students
wouldn't just be mad — they'd be outraged.

"Finally crack down on misbehavior. It's
exactly what we need." Kulbarsh's eyes were
shining. Nothing pleased
him more than an
unpopular plan. "Good
work, Robinson."

CRUD!

My mouth went dry. This was _not_ good. When students heard how their precious gift was spent, they'd go ballistic.

"Dr. Kulbarsh?" I had to do something — _fast_. "Thanks for the suggestions and all, but I'd better try and figure this out myself."

"It's too late." Kulbarsh thumped the desk. "My mind is made up."

"No!" I was frantic.

"NOOOOOOO????" Kulbarsh leaned over his desk, his voice filling the room. "Isn't that what you _wanted_? For me to decide?"

"Yes. _No_," I said miserably.

"Well, I'VE DECIDED," declared Kulbarsh.

How could I have been so stupid? Of course Kulbarsh would come up with some evil plan. When everyone found out I'd turned the decision over to him, who knows what they'd do?

Kulbarsh's eyes drilled into me. "What did you _think_ I'd propose? A waterslide? Slurpee machine? BMX rider in residence? Violent Cartoon Film Festival?"

Miserably, I kicked the floor. I couldn't let this happen! "Dr. Kulbarsh, I know a security camera would be useful, but Mr. Banacek wants us kids to decide. I admit, I was overwhelmed — but that's no reason to give up our rights. I'm up to it! I know I am!"

Kulbarsh rubbed his forehead.

"Okay, Danny." He sighed. "I'll let you decide. But if you can't? Then we get the security camera. Case closed."

YES!

It wasn't until I hit the hallway that the strangeness of our meeting hit me. How did Kulbarsh get me to beg — for the very thing I'd come to get rid of?

Now I had only one more day to decide.

One more day!

I was frantic.
So when Chantal
cornered me in the
hall, I really was not
in the mood.

"Don't even think
about not choosing
my idea," Chantal
said. "Seeing as
how I made you
president..."

I lifted my chin. "I'll do what I think is right."

"If it wasn't for me" — Chantal got right up
in my face — "you wouldn't be president."

"I didn't want to be president," I hissed.
"I'm in this mess because of you! Everyone
thinks I owe them! What do I have to be
grateful for?"

Chantal blinked.

"Don't you <u>want</u> power, Danny?" She seemed honestly puzzled. "I bet you always complained school wasn't made for your type. Too many dumb events, right? And always ruled by jocks, or airheads, or me."

<u>Was I that easy to read?</u>

"Maybe," I mumbled. "But —"

"Now you can do what you want! Have an art supply swap! Panel of comic book artists! Band T-Shirt Day! Hairy eyeball drawing contest!"

<u>Whoa.</u> "Hairy eyeball —?"

"WHATEVS! I'm just saying, don't whine about power, 'cuz it's a gift. Yeah, some people won't like what you decide. Will that kill you?"

I gulped, still thinking about the contest.

"You should definitely pick Middle School Idol, 'cuz it's a straight-up, chart-busting, smokin'-hot idea, and if you don't, I will personally kick your butt. But don't blame me for making you powerful. Too many people in this world have _no_ power. So if you got it, _do_ something with it."

As I walked home, Chantal's challenge lodged in my brain. Of all people, who would think she'd be the one to wake me up?

* CHAPTER TWELVE *

"And here to make the big announcement
is . . . student council president DANNY SHINE!"

My heart was beating so loud, I could barely
hear the audience:

"Paintball!" "Snowflake!" "Middle School Idol!"

Am I really doing this?

I walked onstage and stood next to Kulbarsh.

"Today we're joined by the Royal Order of Porcupines," said Kulbarsh. "They are giving us a generous check, which Danny will accept on the school's behalf. Please welcome their leader, Mr. Bill Banacek!"

Whistles, cheers, and hoots. A bunch of guys in prickly hats stood up and roared. Banacek waved to the crowd like a president in a motorcade. You could tell he was enjoying himself.

Banacek took the mike. "Now, when you hear 'Royal Order of Porcupines,' I know what you're thinking. People are just in it for the secret sword initiation and annual rib dinner. But that's not true!"

I saw Jasper in the audience, rolling his eyes.

"Our mission is to improve the community. So we want to give you, Gerald Ford Middle School, this check for three thousand dollars." Banacek held it up dramatically.

"Woo-hoo!" "Yay!" "Uh-HUH!"

The screams made my stomach twist even more.

"Get a picture of us," Banacek told a photographer at the base of the stage. He steered me to the Porcupines' banner.

"Um, I don't think —" I started.

CLICK! FLASH!

Someone from our school newspaper held up a phone and clicked.

I felt my face redden. All the hoopla was making me even more nervous for my announcement.

"Let's get our Grand Quillmaster up here!" Banacek waved to another red-faced, horn-hatted guy. "Hey, Clyde!"

This was getting worse and worse.

The silver-haired Porcupine leaped onstage. "Let's bring up all the brothers!"

"RAH! RAH! RAH! RAH! RAH!" A second later, there was a stampede of prickly hats.

My head throbbed, and I felt like I was going to burst.

"WILL...YOU...PLEASE...LISTEN?" I shouted.

The cheering stopped.

"Danny," Kulbarsh whispered. "What are you...?"

"I'm sorry," I said. "But we can't accept the money."

Everyone gasped.

Kulbarsh, Banacek, the Porcupines, the audience — all stared like I had two heads.

"W-wh-what?" Banacek cupped his ear.

"We can't accept the money." My voice got louder.

The audience went crazy. "What the —"

"NOOOOOOOO!"

"Who says?"

Kulbarsh's nostrils flared. "May I speak to you . . . offstage?"

I shook my head. "It's better if I explain it to everyone." I turned to Banacek, who looked like he was about to explode.

"When you announced you were giving us this gift," I began, "everyone was excited. It was up to the student council to decide what to do with it. But we couldn't agree on anything."

Banacek huffed. "So?"

"People are always fighting! Half the time, we can't agree on whether to even have a meeting. That's how bad it is."

"But, Danny," Kulbarsh said. "The bylaws say —"

"That it's up to me." I looked at Banacek. "The student council president. Suddenly, I'm the decider. And if I didn't choose the 'right thing,' I was a dead man. You want me to make an impossible decision." I lifted my chin. "But I refuse."

The Porcupines looked baffled. Banacek was sweating and angry. Kulbarsh frowned.

"The group can't come together," I explained. "No one will give an inch. The atmosphere is kind of, well, poisonous. The way I see it is, if we can't agree, then we don't deserve that gift."

"BOO! BOO! BOO!" the audience yelled.

Banacek was still fuming.

"This is . . . it's unbelievable." He threw his arms up. "At a time when _no_ school has enough money, we're offering a nice chunk of change.

AND YOU GUYS CAN'T AGREE ON HOW TO SPEND IT?"

Clyde, the other Porcupine, came over and put his hand on Banacek's shoulder. "Don't sweat it, Bill," he said. "We'll find another school . . ."

Kulbarsh winced like he was in pain. Suddenly, there was a cry like a foghorn from out in the auditorium.

"NOOOOOOOOOOOOOOOOOOOOOOOOO!!!" It was Chantal, sprinting to the podium.

"DON'T GIVE IT TO ANYONE ELSE!" she howled from the base of the stage. "We'll decide! Right here. Right now."

Stunned silence.

"What's everybody looking at?" She turned around and faced the auditorium. "Student council, haul your sorry butts up here, one-two-three. Or I'll <u>kick</u> 'em up."

People got up hesitantly, waiting for Kulbarsh's reaction. The principal cleared his throat.

"You heard the lady," he said.

Yay! Maybe it wasn't totally over.

Seconds later, the entire student council was climbing onstage. The Porcupines moved over to clear space. It was like a crowd scene from the school musical, when I was Third Peasant on the Left.

Kulbarsh pointed to the wings. "Take them backstage. I'm going to continue the assembly. You have . . ." He looked at his watch. "Ten minutes."

Ten minutes?

"That's like asking me to scale Mount Everest in a passing period!" I protested.

"Be a leader, Danny." Kulbarsh's voice was deadly. "This is what a leader does. He leads."

"But —"

"_No buts._" His face was grim. "This is our last chance."

Kulbarsh raced back to the podium. "So sorry about this, uh, glitch, Mr. Banacek." He turned to the audience. "Our next agenda item is — locker tidiness."

The audience groaned. Banacek rolled his eyes.

I took a deep breath and walked backstage to face an angry student council. They were standing up among boxes of props, costumes, and lighting equipment.

I swallowed.

"Everyone, sit down." I tried to steady my voice. "Let's talk about our choices: Paintball. Zombie movie. Battle of the Bands. Snowflake Dance. Middle School Idol. A Thousand Cranes. Bollywood musical." What a weird mash-up.

Ginnifer kicked off the fighting.

"We don't want Paintball Day!" she wailed.

"Well, we don't want a stupid dance!" Tank shot back.

"I'm not asking what you want," I said. "I'm asking what you could live with. Because that's the choice — something you can maybe, possibly, barely tolerate, or — nothing at all."

Silence.

"Go around and say one thing you like about someone else's plan," I said. "Just one."

Everyone looked at me blankly.

"I'll go first," I said. "What I like about Battle of the Bands is . . . hearing guitar solos." I nodded at Ginnifer. "Now you go."

Ginnifer frowned. "I don't mind the idea of a student musical," she said. "But the test-taking theme is weird."

"Good things only," I said, looking at my watch. "So you don't mind the idea of a musical. Who else?"

Eight minutes left.

Axl lifted his chin. "I admit, zombies are cool. Once Danny drew me a mangled, bloody skull tattoo, with brains spilling out. It was totally rude."

We went around the room, one by one. I checked my watch again — three minutes! Glancing over at the stage, I bit my thumbnail. Could I beg for more time?

"Keep going," I yelled as I backed away.

I raced over to the stage and tugged at Kulbarsh again. "We need a few more minutes."

Kulbarsh waved his finger. "No! Bring them back!"

Yikes! I bolted offstage again, nearly hitting a supporting column. Approaching the heavy drapes, I heard snatches of conversation.

"The main character — does she sing?"

"Cool! How do you make the wings flap?"

"Fake blood? I can make <u>fake brains</u>."

Were people actually talking to each other? I peeked behind the curtain and saw unfamiliar pairings:

I poked my head in. "Guys, we're out of time."

"We're almost there, Danny." Chantal wiped her brow.

"I'll try to stall 'em." Turning around, I sprinted for the stage. If I got on the mike and kept talking, they couldn't end the assembly. Then maybe — maybe! — the student council would come up with something.

When I reached the podium, Kulbarsh was making his last announcements. "Turn in your signed permission slips . . ."

As I waited for an opening, Banacek whispered, "Assembly's almost over. You guys blew it."

I looked at the wings — no one.

"When you leave the auditorium," Kulbarsh continued, "please exit in an orderly —"

I tugged the Kulbarsh's sleeve. "Can I just say a few words?" I whispered.

Kulbarsh turned to me with blazing eyes. "The student council!" he whispered angrily. "WHERE ARE THEY?"

    "They're coming!" I glanced into the wings again.

    "Too late," said Kulbarsh.

    Crud!

    I grabbed the mike.

    "Danny! what —?" Kulbarsh sputtered.

    "As student council president, I just want to say..." What? My mind was a complete blank! "Well, good-bye, of course. But before I do, I just want to give a shout-out to someone at this school who needs no introduction..."

Kulbarsh stared, bewildered.

Desperately, I looked around for someone. My eyes landed on a kid with a sandwich, which gave me an idea. "The tall red-haired cafeteria lady..." What was her name? "Doris! Let's give her a round of applause."

Puzzled clapping.

"Because she's really, uh —" Think of something! "Polite. She'll tell you what bok choy is. When you drop your pizza bagel, she'll give you another. One time, she snuck me extra —"

Kulbarsh whispered, "Where is this going?"

"Cantaloupe slices." Just keep talking. "Which reminds me of a movie I saw..."

"Good lord." Kulbarsh sighed.

"About this evil scientist. Dr. Insane? Dr. Nutcase? Something like that. Anyway, he injects his wife with an antiaging serum, and she turns into a giant insect who feasts on human flesh..."

"Wrap it up!" Kulbarsh hissed. "Now!"

"And when a sinister mastermind meets an army of cannibals, you know it's not going to end well..." Get over here, Chantal!

"STOP!" Kulbarsh grabbed the mike out of my hand.

"NO!" I wouldn't give up the mike.

"Sayonara." Banacek saluted us and walked offstage. "I'm _done_."

CRUD!

"Everybody!" Kulbarsh yelled. "Have a safe —"

It was over. All of us had failed — me, the student council, and the school. The overhead lights went on, and people got up to leave. I felt like I had a bag of rocks on my chest.

I started to slump offstage . . .

"NOT SO FAST!"

All heads spun around. Chantal leaped onstage, panting.

"We got it," she said.

* CHAPTER THIRTEEN *

"You mean...?"

"We've got a plan. For the money." Chantal doubled over onstage, trying to catch her breath. "Don't leave."

But Banacek was gone.

"FIND HIM!" Kulbarsh roared. "THE GUY IN THE HAT!"

Holy crud.

I bolted down the stage stairs like an Olympic runner and leaped into the main lobby. Where was he — where? Where? My head was pounding. If only Chantal had come five seconds earlier!

I ran up and down the hall like a madman. "Mr. Banacek! Mr. Banacek!" I yelled. "MISTER BANACEEEEEEEEK!"

But the halls were empty.

Shoulders slumped, I ducked in the bathroom. I could hide here — for a while, anyway. Then something caught my eye.

"Mr. . . . Banacek?" I coughed.

The door swung open and the red-faced Porcupine appeared.

"Danny?"

Holy crud!

"We — they — the student council." I paused to catch my breath. "They did it! They have a plan!"

Banacek shook his head. "I'm sorry, but —"

"No buts," I interrupted. Pulling his sleeve, I opened the bathroom door and led him down the hall.

We hit the auditorium just as the bell rang.

"EVERYONE STAY SEATED!" I commanded, bursting through the double doors. I proudly delivered a prickly-hatted man to the podium, like a hunter bringing home his catch.

The student council was crammed onstage.

"Mr. Banacek." Kulbarsh's eyes lit up.

"YOU'RE BACK! We finally have a proposal!"

Chantal stepped forward.

"Here's what we got," she said. "An original

Bollywood student musical with zombies, paintball

warriors, and heavy-metal music. Cast party with a snowflake theme. Profits go to a children's hospital. Programs printed on special paper, and when the show's over? Fold 'em into origami birds."

Wow. Totally weird, but also kind of perfect.

"I don't know." Banacek scratched his chin.

"Yeah! Woo-hoo!" yelled the audience.

Chantal stared him down. "Now where else are you going to hear a plan as original as _that_?

Banacek nodded. "Let me powwow with the others. Clyde! Vern! Mort!"

The Porcupines came back onstage and huddled. When they finished, Banacek handed me a check.

"Congratulations, Gerald Ford," said Banacek. "Your project sounds, uh, pretty strange. But we're impressed with your democracy in action. We'll give you the check — on one condition."

I looked over at Chantal, worried.

"That we all get tickets," said Banacek, and the guys cheered.

I took the mike. "Let's hear it for the Royal Order of . . ."

"PORCUPINES!!!!" The audience roared.

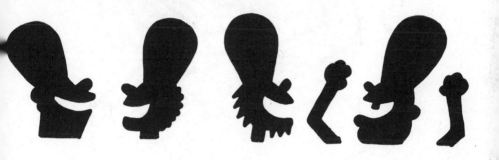

"We did it, Danny! We DID IT!" Chantal slapped my back. Now that the assembly was finally over, everyone crowded onstage, congratulating one another.

"Hey, Chantal." I took her aside, hungry for details. "How did you guys finally agree?"

Chantal lifted her chin.

"It's called horse-trading." She smiled. "Dinesh agreed to make me lead zombie."

I whistled. "Good move."

"You did okay too," she said. "Using your power to kick our butts. You forced us to work it out. I haven't given up on Middle School Idol, though."

"And we haven't given up on Mutant Truckers," Phil said, sticking out his chin. Jasper and Ahmet came up behind him. "We're going to shoot the movie ourselves."

"It's better that way." Ahmet sniffed. "More creative control."

"I'm sorry about —" My eyes landed on Jasper. "You know."

Jasper's mouth twisted, and he looked at the floor. "You were in a tough spot," he admitted. "At least we got Dinesh to make the school administrators into zombies. He made me Director of Severed Limbs."

"Good." I wasn't sure how to get back to normal. "If you really do want to make that movie, we should punch up the script." My eyes slid over to Jasper again.

"Sounds like a plan." He pushed up his glasses. "I'm around all weekend."

"Great," I said, relieved.

YES!

"See you later," I said. "I've got to find someone."

My eyes scanned the area for Asia. Crossing the stage, I overheard Axl talking to Banacek and the Porcupines.

"... about that secret sword initiation." Axl was asking. "How do you become a member? In our club, you have to prove yourself — you know, steal a bike or graffiti a landmark, blow up a toilet . . ."

I tried to pass by without him noticing.

"Hey, Danny!" Axl broke away and grabbed me by the elbow.

"Ow!" My arm hurt.

"We need to rehearse something in the Multi-Purpose Room," he said. "Amundson said you've got the key."

"Oh. Okay." I fished it out of my pocket. "By the way, sorry about Battle of the Bands. Maybe some other time."

"Maybe." Axl shrugged. "Right now, we've got this other gig."

"You mean — the musical?" I asked.

"They want us to do a heavy-metal number." His hands attacked an imaginary guitar. "We're going to tear down the freakin' house."

"Cool."

"Anyway, we don't need a school contest to tell us we're the best band — we know. Who's better? Clown Barf? The Barney Katz Experience?"

I laughed. What had I been so worried about? Everyone had adjusted pretty quickly to the news. In fact, they all claimed to be better off _not_ getting what they wanted.

"Danny?" Kulbarsh walked toward us, and Axl ran.

"Hey." I ducked my head.

Looking at his smile-free face, I couldn't tell if he was still mad. Neither of us spoke for a moment.

"You were sure taking a risk there." Kulbarsh lifted his chin. "Playing King Solomon. But it paid off."

"I'm glad you didn't buy a spy camera," I said.

"I never intended to," he said.

"But you said —"

"I was bluffing." Kulbarsh shrugged. "Trying to wake you up. I hoped you'd take back the decision. So I took a risk too."

wow. "Lucky how it turned out."

"Darn right. In the end, you got them to come together." He sighed. "If only Congress could do that."

I smiled and left the stage to continue my search. If I were Asia, where would I be? I jogged through the hall, wondering if she was at an after-school club. I found myself heading to the music room.

When I poked my head in, I saw a mass of dark hair bent over a brightly colored African drum. She was alone.

"Hey," I said.

"Hey."

I couldn't think of anything to say.

"You —" She blinked. "You surprised me up there. You surprised all of us."

Was that good or bad?

"I was stupid," Asia said. She shook her head disgustedly. "I thought I'd talked you into my idea by _not_ using words. It just seemed like you really got it."

The moment flashed through my mind.

Had I totally blown it?

"I *did* get it." My voice was low. "I wanted to do it too. But I also wanted to force people to come together. It seemed like that was my job."

Was. I'd used the past tense.

"What you did was cool." She gave a disappointed smile. "It took creativity — the same kind you use to draw a smelly sock, or write a zombie movie. In fact, bringing the council together might be the most creative thing you ever did."

I hadn't thought of it that way. "Wow. Huh."

She reached into her messenger bag, and I saw a flash of bright yellow. She pressed another paper bird into my hand.

"Yours," she said.

"See you in the sky," she said mysteriously.

The door opened, and more people came in. I waved good-bye to Asia, my pulse still racing. Feeling a strange stirring in my head, I knew what I had to do.

Malibu was in the student council office when I found her. I knew she'd be there, going over

proofs for the wild
West Barbecue
poster, authorizing
expenditures, or
updating the website.
I used to see her
silhouette from the
hall when I stayed
late after school.

   "It's nacho cheese, not 'macho cheese.'"
She sighed, putting down her red pencil.
   WHAP! CLANG!
   I tossed her a stack of yellow slips
and a key.
   "Danny." Malibu picked up the yellow slips.
"What are these?"
   "Hall passes," I said. "A year's worth. You
could leave class five times a day and get chili
cheese curly fries at the food truck."

"Um —" She frowned.

"But I know you won't," I said. "You're not in it for the hall passes, petty cash, or Media Room key."

Malibu tilted her head, confused.

"Yeah . . . so?"

"So," I said, "you deserve to be president."

Malibu's mouth fell open.

"WHAT?"

"I'm making you president," I said. "It's in the bylaws. 'If the president has to vacate for any reason, due to relocation, illness, or failure to meet academic standards...'" I read from the pamphlet.

"Are you moving?" Malibu's eyes widened. "Flunking? Did you sprain your drawing finger? Get suspended for tattooing the school statue?"

"Nope."

"Then why...?"

I sat down.

"Student council always sounded like a drag. And it can be, but — now I get that it's worth doing. You can't whine that school reeks and never try to change it. Then you've lost complaining rights."

"So why resign?" Malibu wrinkled her nose.

"Because the job is what you make it," I went on. "If you're Dex, you do the minimum and nothing changes. Someone else — who's supersmart, experienced, and really cares — could totally turn things around. I'm not that person. But I think you are."

Malibu's cheeks flushed.

"I'll still go to meetings," I said. "I want to get this musical off the ground."

"You know..." Malibu smiled shyly. "I always wanted the job. But I hated coming up with stupid slogans and handing out candy bars."

"Now you don't have to." I stood up. "Congratulations, Madame President."

She smiled.

Walking down the hall a few minutes later, I felt ten times lighter. Now I could leave on a high note. Suddenly, someone grabbed me from behind and put me in a headlock. Ow!

"Let go, Axl," I said. The arm relaxed, and I squirmed free.

But it wasn't Axl. Instead, Bruiser Pekarsky stood there.

WOODCHUCK FOOTBALL

"Hey, Shine," he said. "Too bad we never got to wrestle."

"Yeah." I coughed. "Too bad."

"Luckily, there's a make-up tournament," he

said. "Cuz so many people missed the first one. Awesome, huh?"

CRUD!

He gave me a crooked smile. Then he punched me in the arm and walked away, chuckling.

I had to fight Bruiser after all? Avoiding him was why I'd run for president! I can't wrestle him, I thought. It's impossible. On the other hand — I never thought I could bring the student council together. Who knew what I could do?

I called out after him.

Bring it on.

<u>H.N. KOWITT</u> has written more than fifty books for younger readers, including The Loser List series, Dracula's Decomposition Book, This Book Is a Joke, and The Sweetheart Deal. She lives in New York City, where she enjoys cycling, flea markets, and gardening on her windowsill. You can find her online at www.kowittbooks.com.

Danny Shine just wants to draw comics, buy comics, and talk about comics. But first, he has to get his name off of

Read them all!

When the new guy threatens Danny's comic-drawing dreams, it's time for

Danny broke out of his loser shell. But can he break the